A Dinner at Poplar Walk

Charles Dickens

This is a work of fiction. Names, characters, organizations, places, events, and incidents are either products of the author's imagination or are used fictitiously. Any resemblance of actual persons, living or dead, or actual events is purely coincidental.

No part of this work may be reproduced, or stored in a retrieval system, or transmitted in any form or by any means, electronic, mechanical, photocopying, recording, or otherwise, without express permission of the publisher.

A Dinner at Poplar Walk by Charles Dickens
First Published: 1833
Cover Image: An Evening Party
Artist: George Cruikshank
Date: 1826
Credit Line: MET Museum
License: CC0 1.0 Universal (CC0 1.0)

Published by Digibooks OOD / Demetra Publishing, Bulgaria.

All rights reserved.

Contact: info@demetrapublishing.com

ISBN: 9798618344319

A DINNER AT POPLAR WALK

Mr. Augustus Minns was a bachelor, of about forty as he said — of about eight-and-forty as his friends said. He was always exceedingly clean, precise, and tidy; perhaps somewhat priggish, and the most retiring man in the world. He usually wore a brown frock-coat without a wrinkle, light inexplicables without a spot, a neat neckerchief with a remarkably neat tie, and boots without a fault; moreover, he always carried a brown silk umbrella with an ivory handle. He was a clerk in Somerset-house, or, as he said himself, he held 'a responsible situation under Government.' He had a good and increasing salary, in addition to some 10,000*l.* of his own (invested in the funds), and he occupied a first floor in Tavistock-street, Covent-garden, where he had resided for twenty years, having been in the habit of quarrelling with his landlord the whole time: regularly giving notice of his intention to quit on the first day of every quarter, and as regularly countermanding it on the second. There were two classes of created objects which he held in the deepest and most unmingled horror; these were dogs, and children. He was not unamiable, but he could, at any time, have viewed the execution of a dog, or the assassination of an infant, with the liveliest satisfaction. Their habits were at variance with his love of order; and his love of order was as powerful as his love of life. Mr. Augustus Minns had no relations, in or near London, with the exception of his cousin, Mr. Octavius Budden, to whose son, whom he had never seen (for he disliked the father), he had consented to become godfather by proxy. Mr. Budden having realised a moderate fortune by exercising the trade or calling of a corn-chandler, and having a great predilection for the country, had purchased a cottage in the vicinity of Stamford-hill, whither he retired with the wife of his bosom, and his only son, Master Alexander Augustus Budden. One evening, as Mr. and Mrs. B. were admiring their son, discussing his various merits, talking over his education, and disputing whether the classics should be made an essential part thereof, the lady pressed so strongly upon her husband the propriety of cultivating the friendship of Mr. Minns in behalf of their son, that Mr. Budden at last made up his mind, that it should not be his fault if he and his cousin were not in future more intimate.

'I'll break the ice, my love,' said Mr. Budden, stirring up the sugar at the bottom of his glass of brandy-and-water, and casting a sidelong look at his spouse to see the effect of the announcement of his determination, 'by asking Minns down to dine with us, on Sunday.'

'Then pray, Budden, write to your cousin at once,' replied Mrs. Budden. 'Who knows, if we could only get him down here, but he might take a fancy to our Alexander, and leave him his property? — Alick, my dear, take your legs off the rail of the chair!'

'Very true,' said Mr. Budden, musing, 'very true indeed, my love!' On the following morning, as Mr. Minns was sitting at his breakfast-table, alternately biting his dry toast and casting a look upon the columns of his morning paper, which he always read from the title to the printer's name, he heard a loud knock at the street-door; which was shortly afterwards followed by the entrance of his servant, who put into his hands a particularly small card, on which was engraven in immense letters, 'Mr. Octavius Budden, Amelia Cottage (Mrs. B.'s name was Amelia), Poplar-walk, Stamford-hill.'

'Budden!' ejaculated Minns, 'what can bring that vulgar man here! — say I'm asleep — say I'm out, and shall never be home again — anything to keep him down-stairs.'

'But please, sir, the gentleman's coming up,' replied the servant, and the fact was made evident, by an appalling creaking of boots on the staircase accompanied by a pattering noise; the cause of which, Minns could not, for the life of him, divine.

'Hem — show the gentleman in,' said the unfortunate bachelor. Exit servant, and enter Octavius preceded by a large white dog, dressed in a suit of fleecy hosiery, with pink eyes, large ears, and no perceptible tail.

The cause of the pattering on the stairs was but too plain. Mr. Augustus Minns staggered beneath the shock of the dog's appearance.

'My dear fellow, how are you?' said Budden, as he entered.

He always spoke at the top of his voice, and always said the same thing half-a-dozen times.

'How are you, my hearty?'

'How do you do, Mr. Budden? — pray take a chair!' politely stammered the discomfited Minns.

'Thank you — thank you — well — how are you, eh?'

'Uncommonly well, thank you,' said Minns, casting a diabolical look at the dog, who, with his hind legs on the floor, and his fore paws resting on the table, was dragging a bit of bread and butter out of a plate, preparatory to devouring it, with the buttered side next the carpet.

'Ah, you rogue!' said Budden to his dog; 'you see, Minns, he's like me, always at home, eh, my boy! — Egad, I'm precious hot and hungry! I've walked all the way from Stamford-hill this morning.'

'Have you breakfasted?' inquired Minns.

'Oh, no! — came to breakfast with you; so ring the bell, my dear fellow, will you? and let's have another cup and saucer, and the cold ham. — Make myself at home, you see!' continued Budden, dusting his boots with a table-napkin. 'Ha! — ha! — ha!— 'pon my life, I'm hungry.'

Minns rang the bell, and tried to smile.

'I decidedly never was so hot in my life,' continued Octavius, wiping his forehead; 'well, but how are you, Minns? 'Pon my soul, you wear capitally!'

'D'ye think so?' said Minns; and he tried another smile.

"Pon my life, I do!'

'Mrs. B. and — what's his name — quite well?'

'Alick — my son, you mean; never better — never better. But at such a place as we've got at Poplar-walk, you know, he couldn't be ill if he tried. When I first saw it, by Jove! it looked so knowing, with the front garden, and the green railings and the brass knocker, and all that — I really thought it was a cut above me.'

'Don't you think you'd like the ham better,' interrupted Minns, 'if you cut it the other way?' He saw, with feelings which it is impossible to describe, that his visitor was cutting or rather maiming the ham, in utter violation of all established rules.

'No, thank ye,' returned Budden, with the most barbarous indifference to crime, 'I prefer it this way, it eats short. But I say, Minns, when will you come down and see us? You will be delighted with the place; I know you will. Amelia and I were talking about you the other night, and Amelia said — another lump of sugar, please; thank ye — she said, don't you think you could contrive, my dear, to say to Mr. Minns, in a friendly way — come down, sir — damn the dog! he's spoiling your curtains, Minns — ha! — ha! — ha!' Minns leaped from his seat as though he had received the discharge from a galvanic battery.

'Come out, sir! — go out, hoo!' cried poor Augustus, keeping, nevertheless, at a very respectful distance from the dog; having read of a case of hydrophobia in the paper of that morning. By dint of great exertion, much shouting, and a marvellous deal of poking under the tables with a stick and umbrella, the dog was at last dislodged, and placed on the landing outside the door, where he immediately commenced a most appalling howling; at the same time vehemently scratching the paint off the two nicely-varnished bottom panels, until they resembled the interior of a backgammon-board.

'A good dog for the country that!' coolly observed Budden to the distracted Minns, 'but he's not much used to confinement. But now, Minns, when will you come down? I'll take no denial, positively. Let's see, to-day's Thursday. —

Will you come on Sunday? We dine at five, don't say no — do.'

After a great deal of pressing, Mr. Augustus Minns, driven to despair, accepted the invitation, and promised to be at Poplar-walk on the ensuing Sunday, at a quarter before five to the minute.

'Now mind the direction,' said Budden: 'the coach goes from the Flower-pot, in Bishopsgate-street, every half hour. When the coach stops at the Swan, you'll see, immediately opposite you, a white house.'

'Which is your house — I understand,' said Minns, wishing to cut short the visit, and the story, at the same time.

'No, no, that's not mine; that's Grogus's, the great ironmonger's. I was going to say — you turn down by the side of the white house till you can't go another step further — mind that! — and then you turn to your right, by some stables — well; close to you, you'll see a wall with "Beware of the Dog" written on it in large letters — (Minns shuddered) — go along by the side of that wall for about a quarter of a mile — and anybody will show you which is my place.'

'Very well — thank ye — good-bye.'

'Be punctual.'

'Certainly: good morning.'

'I say, Minns, you've got a card.'

'Yes, I have; thank ye.' And Mr. Octavius Budden departed, leaving his cousin looking forward to his visit on the following Sunday, with the feelings of a penniless poet to the weekly visit of his Scotch landlady.

Sunday arrived; the sky was bright and clear; crowds of people were hurrying along the streets, intent on their different schemes of pleasure for the day; everything and everybody looked cheerful and happy except Mr. Augustus Minns.

The day was fine, but the heat was considerable; when Mr. Minns had fagged up the shady side of Fleet-street, Cheapside, and Threadneedle-street, he had become pretty warm, tolerably dusty, and it was getting late into the bargain. By the most extraordinary good fortune, however, a coach was waiting at the Flower-pot, into which

Mr. Augustus Minns got, on the solemn assurance of the cad that the vehicle would start in three minutes — that being the very utmost extremity of time it was allowed to wait by Act of Parliament. A quarter of an hour elapsed, and there were no signs of moving. Minns looked at his watch for the sixth time.

'Coachman, are you going or not?' bawled Mr. Minns, with his head and half his body out of the coach window.

'Di-rectly, sir,' said the coachman, with his hands in his pockets, looking as much unlike a man in a hurry as possible.

'Bill, take them cloths off.' Five minutes more elapsed: at the end of which time the coachman mounted the box, from whence he looked down the street, and up the street, and hailed all the pedestrians for another five minutes.

'Coachman! if you don't go this moment, I shall get out,' said Mr. Minns, rendered desperate by the lateness of the hour, and the impossibility of being in Poplar-walk at the appointed time.

'Going this minute, sir,' was the reply; — and, accordingly, the machine trundled on for a couple of hundred yards, and then stopped again. Minns doubled himself up in a corner of the coach, and abandoned himself to his fate, as a child, a mother, a bandbox and a parasol, became his fellow-passengers.

The child was an affectionate and an amiable infant; the little dear mistook Minns for his other parent, and screamed to embrace him.

'Be quiet, dear,' said the mamma, restraining the impetuosity of the darling, whose little fat legs were kicking, and stamping, and twining themselves into the most complicated forms, in an ecstasy of impatience. 'Be quiet, dear, that's not your papa.'

'Thank Heaven I am not!' thought Minns, as the first gleam of pleasure he had experienced that morning shone like a meteor through his wretchedness.

Playfulness was agreeably mingled with affection in the disposition of the boy. When satisfied that Mr. Minns was not his parent, he endeavoured to attract his notice by scraping his drab trousers with his dirty shoes, poking his chest with his mamma's parasol, and other nameless endearments peculiar to infancy, with which he beguiled the tediousness of the ride, apparently very much to his own satisfaction.

When the unfortunate gentleman arrived at the Swan, he found to his great dismay, that it was a quarter past five. The white house, the stables, the 'Beware of the Dog,' — every landmark was passed, with a rapidity not unusual to a gentleman of a certain age when too late for dinner. After the lapse of a few minutes, Mr. Minns found himself opposite a yellow brick house with a green door, brass knocker, and door-plate, green window-frames and ditto railings, with 'a garden' in front, that is to say, a small loose bit of gravelled ground, with one round and two scalene triangular beds, containing a fir-tree, twenty or thirty bulbs, and an unlimited number of marigolds. The taste of Mr. and Mrs. Budden was further displayed by the appearance of a Cupid on each side of the door, perched upon a heap of large chalk flints, variegated with pink conch-shells. His knock at the door was answered by a stumpy boy, in drab livery, cotton stockings and high-lows, who, after hanging his hat on one of the dozen brass pegs which ornamented the passage, denominated by courtesy 'The Hall,' ushered him into a front drawing-room commanding a very extensive view of the backs of the neighbouring houses. The usual ceremony of introduction, and so forth, over, Mr. Minns took his seat: not a little agitated at finding that he was the last comer, and, somehow or other, the Lion of about a dozen people, sitting together in a small drawing-room, getting rid of that most tedious of all time, the time preceding dinner.

'Well, Brogson,' said Budden, addressing an elderly gentleman in a black coat, drab knee-breeches, and long gaiters, who, under pretence of inspecting the prints in an Annual, had been engaged in satisfying himself on the subject of Mr. Minns's general appearance, by looking at him over the tops of the leaves— 'Well, Brogson, what do ministers mean to do? Will they go out, or what?'

'Oh — why — really, you know, I'm the last person in the world to ask for news. Your cousin, from his situation, is the most likely person to answer the question.'

Mr. Minns assured the last speaker, that although he was in Somerset-house, he possessed no official communication relative to the projects of his Majesty's Ministers. But his remark was evidently received incredulously; and no further conjectures being hazarded on the subject, a long pause ensued, during which the company occupied themselves in coughing and blowing their noses, until the entrance of Mrs. Budden caused a general rise.

The ceremony of introduction being over, dinner was announced, and down-stairs the party proceeded accordingly — Mr. Minns escorting Mrs. Budden as far as the drawing-room door, but being prevented, by the narrowness of the staircase, from extending his gallantry any farther. The dinner passed off as such dinners usually do. Ever and anon, amidst the clatter of knives and forks, and the hum of conversation, Mr. B.'s voice might be heard, asking a friend to take wine, and assuring him he was glad to see him; and a great deal of by-play took place between Mrs. B. and the servants, respecting the removal of the dishes, during which her countenance assumed all the variations of a weather-glass, from 'stormy' to 'set fair.'

Upon the dessert and wine being placed on the table, the servant, in compliance with a significant look from Mrs. B., brought down 'Master Alexander,' habited in a sky-blue suit with silver buttons; and possessing hair of nearly the same colour as the metal. After sundry praises from his mother, and various admonitions as to his behaviour from his father, he was introduced to his godfather.

'Well, my little fellow — you are a fine boy, ain't you?' said Mr. Minns, as happy as a tomtit on birdlime.

'Yes.'

'How old are you?'

'Eight, next We'nsday. How old are *you?*'

'Alexander,' interrupted his mother, 'how dare you ask Mr. Minns how old he is!'

'He asked me how old *I* was,' said the precocious child, to whom Minns had from that moment internally resolved that he never would bequeath one shilling. As soon as the titter occasioned by the observation had subsided, a little smirking man with red whiskers, sitting at the bottom of the table, who during the whole of dinner had been endeavouring to obtain a listener to some stories about Sheridan, called, out, with a very patronising air, 'Alick, what part of speech is *be*.'

'A verb.'

'That's a good boy,' said Mrs. Budden, with all a mother's pride.

'Now, you know what a verb is?'

'A verb is a word which signifies to be, to do, or to suffer; as, I am — I rule — I am ruled. Give me an apple, Ma.'

'I'll give you an apple,' replied the man with the red whiskers, who was an established friend of the family, or in other words was always invited by Mrs. Budden, whether Mr. Budden liked it or not, 'if you'll tell me what is the meaning of *be*.'

'Be?' said the prodigy, after a little hesitation— 'an insect that gathers honey.'

'No, dear,' frowned Mrs. Budden; 'B double E is the substantive.'

'I don't think he knows much yet about *common* substantives,' said the smirking gentleman, who thought this an admirable opportunity for letting off a joke. 'It's clear he's not very well acquainted with *proper names.* He! he! he!'

'Gentlemen,' called out Mr. Budden, from the end of the table, in a stentorian voice, and with a very important air, 'will you have the goodness to charge your glasses? I have a toast to propose.'

'Hear! hear!' cried the gentlemen, passing the decanters. After they had made the round of the table, Mr. Budden proceeded— 'Gentlemen; there is an individual present—'

'Hear! hear!' said the little man with red whiskers.

'*Pray* be quiet, Jones,' remonstrated Budden.

'I say, gentlemen, there is an individual present,' resumed the host, 'in whose society, I am sure we must take great delight — and — and — the conversation of that individual must have afforded to every one present, the utmost pleasure.' ['Thank Heaven, he does not mean me!' thought Minns, conscious that his diffidence and exclusiveness had prevented his saying above a dozen words since he entered the house.] 'Gentlemen, I am but a humble individual myself, and I perhaps ought to apologise for allowing any individual feeling of friendship and affection for the person I allude to, to induce me to venture to rise, to propose the health of that person — a person that, I am sure — that is to say, a person whose virtues must endear him to those who know him — and those who have not the pleasure of knowing him, cannot dislike him.'

'Hear! hear!' said the company, in a tone of encouragement and approval.

'Gentlemen,' continued Budden, 'my cousin is a man who — who is a relation of my own.' (Hear! hear!) Minns groaned audibly. 'Who I am most happy to see here, and who, if he were not here, would certainly have deprived us of the great pleasure we all feel in seeing him. (Loud cries of hear!) Gentlemen, I feel that I have already trespassed on your attention for too long a time. With every feeling — of — with every sentiment of — of—'

'Gratification' — suggested the friend of the family.

' — Of gratification, I beg to propose the health of Mr. Minns.'

'Standing, gentlemen!' shouted the indefatigable little man with the whiskers— 'and with the honours. Take your time from me, if you please. Hip! hip! hip! — Za! — Hip! hip! hip! — Za! — Hip hip! — Za-a-a!'

All eyes were now fixed on the subject of the toast, who by gulping down port wine at the imminent hazard of suffocation, endeavoured to conceal his confusion. After as long a pause as decency would admit, he rose, but, as the newspapers sometimes say in their reports, 'we regret that we are quite unable to give even the substance of the honourable gentleman's observations.' The words 'present company — honour — present occasion,' and 'great happiness' — heard occasionally, and repeated at intervals, with a countenance expressive of the utmost confusion and misery, convinced the company that he was making an excellent speech; and, accordingly, on his resuming his seat, they cried 'Bravo!' and manifested tumultuous applause. Jones, who had been long watching his opportunity, then darted up.

'Budden,' said he, 'will you allow *me* to propose a toast?'

'Certainly,' replied Budden, adding in an under-tone to Minns right across the table, 'Devilish sharp fellow that: you'll be very much pleased with his speech. He talks equally well on any subject.' Minns bowed, and Mr. Jones proceeded:

'It has on several occasions, in various instances, under many circumstances, and in different companies, fallen to my lot to propose a toast to those by whom, at the time, I have had the honour to be surrounded, I have sometimes, I will cheerfully own — for why should I deny it? — felt the overwhelming nature of the task I have undertaken, and my own utter incapability to do justice to the subject. If such have been my feelings, however, on former occasions, what must they be now — now — under the extraordinary circumstances in which I am placed. (Hear! hear!) To describe my feelings accurately, would be impossible; but I cannot give you a better idea of them, gentlemen, than by referring to a circumstance which happens, oddly enough, to occur to my mind at the moment. On one occasion, when that truly great and illustrious man, Sheridan, was—'

Now, there is no knowing what new villainy in the form of a joke would have been heaped on the grave of that very ill-used man, Mr. Sheridan, if the boy in drab had not at that moment entered the room in a breathless state, to report that, as it was a very wet night, the nine o'clock stage had come round, to know whether there was anybody going to town, as, in that case, he (the nine o'clock) had room for one inside.

Mr. Minns started up; and, despite countless exclamations of surprise, and entreaties to stay, persisted in his determination to accept the vacant place. But, the brown silk umbrella was nowhere to be found; and as the coachman couldn't wait, he drove back to the Swan, leaving word for Mr. Minns to 'run round' and catch him. However, as it did not occur to Mr. Minns for some ten minutes or so, that he had left the brown silk umbrella with the ivory handle in the other coach, coming down; and, moreover, as he was by no means remarkable for speed, it is no matter of surprise that when he accomplished the feat of 'running round' to the Swan, the coach — the last coach — had gone without him.

It was somewhere about three o'clock in the morning, when Mr. Augustus Minns knocked feebly at the street-door of his lodgings in Tavistock-street, cold, wet, cross, and miserable. He made his will next morning, and his professional man informs us, in that strict confidence in which we inform the public, that neither the name of Mr. Octavius Budden, nor of Mrs. Amelia Budden, nor of Master Alexander Augustus Budden, appears therein.

Printed in Great Britain
by Amazon